A Peculiar Day in the Douro Valley

and other stories

A Peculiar Day in the Douro Valley
and other stories

Benjamin Eric

Querencia Press, LLC
Chicago Illinois

QUERENCIA PRESS

© Copyright 2024
Benjamin Eric

ISBN 978 1 959118 90 9

www.querenciapress.com

First Published in 2024

Querencia Press, LLC
Chicago IL

Printed & Bound in the United States of America

To my father, who has always acted in my best interest, especially when I was too young to realize or appreciate those efforts.

To my mother, who died before she got to read these stories. It's been over eight years and we still miss you.

And, of course, my wife, Dana. There is no one I'd rather spend my time with. I owe the joy in my life to you.

Table of Contents

WTMMG

He never drives with the window open. Today he does.

The weather is pleasant. It is rare for temperature to have a perfect balance, whether you are measuring in Celsius or Fahrenheit.

The old neighborhood is green. Radiance from the lush vines is juxtaposed to the city's concrete, and the sprouting nature gives the gray and black blocks an illusion of invisibility.

His friend's music plays through his speakers. One hand is out the window with spread fingers to let the breeze slip through like a stroke in the ocean. Tires roll through memories of their youth. He exerts the speakers to make sure psychedelic sounds can travel, because he knows sound is not similar to light, which is so fast it defines our sense of instant. He wants to make sure the music can travel no matter how slowly.

Perhaps it moves so slowly that it can fade to the past.

Perhaps the music will crawl back fifteen years and meet the two boys in their youth and intersect at a particular moment in their lives. Even if the sound is faint to the point of being mute, maybe they will still hear a whisper that will plant the seed for the song to bloom.

Does the present own a collage of sounds that crawled back from the future?

He brakes at the corner where the two boys would catch the city bus to their special education school. The catholic school kids would laugh and call them retards. Back then, 'learning difference' was the politically correct term for the neurodivergent. The normal kids did not care.

In his car, beside the bus stop, he turns the volume dial to the limit. He plays "WTMMG" (Will This Make Me Good). If sounds can travel through time, he hopes the boys hear that song. Maybe that is what gave them the confidence to give the finger to the catholic school boys who got off four stops before them.

###

Despite the nice weather, he lies in bed. He is tired. "G.O.M.D." (Get Off My Dick) plays and a hush proceeds the fading instrumentals.

His room is quiet. He tries to listen.

There are noises he hears. There are a few he can't identify, like creaks in the house.

Maybe, he thinks, they are from footsteps that belong to whoever will live in this house someday. Will he still live here years from now? Is he hearing himself walk in the other room?

He squints his eyelids and forms a droplet in his socket. He tenses the muscles around his brows, creating a prism of light patterns like a crystal sitting under the lingering sun.

The sun is over ninety-three million miles away from him. He continues to play with the light.

Because light is not like sound. Light is not slow.

Light gives us our concept of instant.

12

A Peculiar Day in the Douro Valley

Paco sat outside his cottage with the vines that grew in his terrace dangling above him. He sipped his espresso as the morning sun rose over Pinhao. The Douro Valley labor harvested the grapes in the morning before the summer heat rose to unbearable temperatures. Even this early in the day, Paco wore his shirt unbuttoned, his bare chest breathing the valley air. The hairs on his chest curled.

The hills of alternating green and brown portrayed various textures depending on the time of day or the direction he looked. Clumps of trees scattered across the hills bore ripe dates. Paco enjoyed watching the automobiles as the drivers cut the wheels to make the sharp turns on the valley roads.

This was Paco's second year in Pinhao. His cottage was rustic, isolated, and, to his liking, intimate. He had a minimalist approach to the interior, since he had only brought a few of his possessions over from Oviedo. Nothing he owned, however, predated the civil war. There was nothing he kept from his childhood in northern Spain other than his memories of running through the streets near the Cathedral of San Salvador. His identity, he felt, was not cultivated from childhood but born from the blood, bones, and intestines that he witnessed scattered across grass and stone.

Inside, he kept his uniform from the war in a locked trunk, with the exception of his boots that he placed to the side. While his rifle had no ammunition, only in his possession as a memento, his pistol always had a full magazine ready to be cocked to load a bullet in the chamber. Those firearms came into his possession when the Siege of Oviedo began and they served him until Franco won the war.

Paco's most cherished possession that he brought from Spain dwarfed the value he designated to his wartime relics. During the years when the wars, which would dictate the successes and failures of ambitious empires, were beginning to dwindle, and as citizens of the world witnessed climaxes featuring the final falling bombs and the fading echoes of flying bullets, Paco acquired his best friend.

Humo ran from inside and snuggled himself beside Paco's leg. Humo's beige hair curled like springs on a springboard and hid his wild eyes. The white on his chest resembled spilled paint. Saliva dripped from his dangling tongue as he panted.

Paco acquired Humo from a farmer who specialized in breeding Spanish Water Dogs who could herd sheep. While Paco had no sheep to herd (his only other animal was a horse named Alfonso), he admired the grace and athleticism of the canine breed. They were short with goofy hair like a child whose parents neglected to groom, but there was a nobility to them. They moved with agility and kept their heads held up with a confidence that was more common with Bengals and Cobras or other predators who had wicked abilities to hunt and maul down their prey.

"It is too hot today," Humo said. "This is the hottest day I can remember."

"You said that yesterday," Paco told his dog.

"I don't remember saying that."

Humo nuzzled his snout against Paco's foot. He reached down and stroked Humo's back, the curls popped up from under his palm and between his fingers.

"I am going down into town later. Is there anything you want me to get for you for when I return?"

"Yes, Guardián. There is something you can do for me," Humo said. He looked up from where he had rested his head, but was unable to make eye contact due to the hair obstructing his eyes. "You can bring me the corpse of that vulgar vulture."

Paco rolled his eyes. Humo had claimed he saw an Egyptian Vulture a few days ago. While native to the Iberian peninsula, Paco did not believe that Humo saw one in the valley so close to the Douro River.

Paco stood up and began buttoning his shirt. His hair was already combed, and he decided to let his five o'clock shadow cast over his face for the day. In the silence of the valley, he took a final sip of his morning espresso, and he could hear the hands of his watch tick as he brought his wrist up near his face.

"It is unlikely that I will be able to bring you that bird when I return."

"I see. Well, Guardián, I will make a promise to you. I will slay that vile scavenger and I will bring its carcass to your feet as a worthy tribute."

"Why so much animosity for that bird?"

"It's a repugnant thing. I once saw it eat dung."

"So? I've seen you eat dung."

Humo huffed. "One time that happened."

Paco rode Alfonso down the dirt roads, where he could roll down for what would seem like eternity if his horse decided to buck and throw him from the saddle. The prospect of falling did not frighten Paco, who flew SM.81's during the war. He had flown over Barcelona alongside the Legionary Air Force. If flying a mechanical vehicle from thousands of feet in the air could not frighten Paco, a horse on a narrow valley would not either.

Whenever he looked down the valley, and across the river, at the hills of alternating brown and green, he thought of Barcelona. The sight reminded him of the city's grid when he looked out the window as his plane soared. He saw the debris and smoke gather in clumps. Even though he was right over the city, it felt as if he was an entire odyssey away. The sounds from the explosion could barely reach him. He was so far removed from the cacophony of war. He was too high up in the clouds to hear the chaos of wailing widows beside maimed men as they attempted to save the lives of now crippled children.

After the first barrage, Paco spoke with the same men who had educated him on the SM.81's controls. They had always been polite to him in their instructions and were patient as they tried to navigate the language barrier between their native Italian and what they could grasp from Spanish. Paco described the noises he heard, and the Italians in the platoon told him that his description was identical to their experience in Guernica.

These memories stayed with Paco until he reached the town and hitched his horse outside Rufete Restaurante, where the white awning contrasted with the establishment's name written in black. He took off his hat and fanned his clammy face and sweat-drenched pits before walking through the door. The clamoring inside among friends, along with the tapping of silverware against plates that held local delicacies, was louder to him than the bombs he dropped. This was a pleasant oasis for him.

Patricia, the owner's daughter, was hosting as she normally did. She recognized everyone from town, including Paco. They exchanged platonic pecks on each cheek as they greeted one another. She had always been patient with Paco's imperfect Portuguese.

"You didn't bring the silly rascal with you?" she asked.

"I left him at home. He was being a bit chatty today."

Patricia laughed. "He's always trying to tell us something and gets irritated when we don't listen."

Paco was ready to take his seat at his usual table under the black and white framed photograph of women stomping on grapes. He was ready to order the Mariscada with a perfect pairing of white wine that was harvested just half a mile away. Before he could go on with the routine, Patricia gripped his arm.

"These two Germans came by looking for you. An older, married couple."

"Germans here?" Paco asked. "What happened? Were all the flights from Berlin to Brazil booked?"

"They specifically asked for you."

"For me?"

Patricia nodded. She anticipated Paco's next question, and told him she did not know why they inquired for him.

"They are staying at the inn just a few doors down," she said. "At least, that is what they told me. They ate here and left about fifteen minutes ago."

"Maybe I can catch them," Paco said. "Excuse me, please. My apologies, darling."

Paco ran outside and past Alfonso. He knew which inn Patricia had referred to and he also knew the proprietors as well as the workers. The bell dinged as he opened the door.

"Excuse me, sir," he said to the man behind the counter. "I do not mean to pry or make a request of you that would leave you in a position to make an unprofessional decision. But I heard an older German couple is inquiring about my whereabouts."

The clerk smiled. "Ah, yes. The Schmitzs. They were asking about you. I believe they may have looked up your address in the directory."

"Do you know when they will be back?"

"They won't. They checked out before they left."

Paco left the inn. He was hungry but dumbfounded with the idea of Germans looking for him. He had not even seen a German since the thirties. Not since he left Spain.

Still bewildered, Paco mounted Alfonso and rode back to his cottage without eating. He did not rush on his travels back, but he did not idle either. This was the first time he traveled on these roads without the memories of Barcelona clinging to his thoughts.

He came home expecting the German couple to be waiting for him. No one was there, however. Just Humo patrolling outside, sniffing about. When he saw Paco he ran over with his rear end wagging with vigor.

"Guardián, I kept the house secure."

"Humo, did any Germans come by here looking for me?"

"Germans? Why would they be here? Were all the flights to Brazil booked?"

Paco let out an abrupt, quick laugh. "Ha! I made that same joke."

The morning ended and still no German couple came to his door. Paco made breakfast and fed Humo. Whatever fish he didn't finish, he placed on the floor to let Humo devour. It was when he watched Humo eat that he realized he did not pray before his meal. A crucifix hung beside his door and he looked at the symbol as he made the sign of the cross and kissed his knuckle.

A mirror hung above the sink, right beside the window that looked out towards the valley. As he washed his plates, his eyes darted back and forth from the vines growing in the hills to his own reflection.

"What do you think of this little bit of facial hair?" he asked Humo.

"You look handsome with that scruff."

"I am not sure. I might shave it."

"You will look handsome clean shaven."

"During the war, I had a mustache. I might regrow that."

"You will look handsome with a mustache."

Paco turned around and bent down to stroke Humo's snout. His entire rear wagged as his legs bounced. Humo's panting breath hit Paco's face. The hot air made his perspiration worse and so he slid off his unbuttoned shirt onto the floor.

"Outside! Outside!" Humo shouted as he adjusted and shifted his ears. "Something is outside!"

Paco looked through the kitchen window. A man and a woman stood outside with the wineries in the backdrop. The charcoal threads they wore were an ugly contrast to all the vibrant green around them. Looking at their clothes made Paco feel overheated. Beside them was a duffel bag.

The couple stood shoulder to shoulder, their height exactly the same when standing on an equal plane. Their hair was the same shade of gray with whorls of black, even though the woman appeared younger. When Paco stepped outside, they smiled and waved at him with such familiarity. Neither the man nor the woman seemed bothered by Humo's howling that echoed from the house.

"Greetings, friend," the man called out. His German accent was prominent. "Pardon us. I hope we are not interrupting your afternoon. We are new to the area and were looking for a friend."

"Are we friends?" Paco asked. "My apologies if my memory is failing me. I do not know too many Germans."

"Please forgive our rudeness for not introducing ourselves. This is my wife, Erikah Schmitz. And I am Benno, of Berlin. You may have known our son, Ernst."

Humo ran out the door with his tail straight back and his snout pointing forward.

"Tell these Nazis to get lost," Humo hollered.

"That is a beautiful canine," Erikah complimented.

"Your flattery is wasted on me." He looked up and glared at Paco through the curls that covered his eyes. "Say the word and I'll tear them apart."

Paco reached into his pocket and pulled out a pack of cigarettes. He put one to his lips and patted his pockets for matches. Humo began yelling at his guardian to watch out, but Paco did not see Benno approach the two of them. Benno had reached into his pocket and pulled out what looked like the grip of a pistol. Paco froze, with the cigarette stuck hanging from his dry lips.

Benno held a light in his hands, the metal case the size of a stone. The flame stood upright, like a soldier in formation before a march. Paco leaned his head forward and listened to the sizzle of his now lit smoke. Engraved into the metal, Paco noticed the swastika.

Similar to a sleight of hand trick, Benno put the light back in his jacket pocket and pulled out a newspaper clipping, a seamless switch of the two objects.

"Is this you?" Benno asked.

Paco grabbed the parchment. The paper had browned and it reminded Paco of rotting flesh. The black ink was more difficult to read over the darkened paper, but with squinted eyes he could still read the story. The writer wrote in Spanish and used descriptors like brave and resilient in the text below the headline that contained Paco's name.

"Is that you they talk about in the paper?" Benno asked again.

"Yes," Paco admitted. "Do you two want to come in for a drink? I have some wine."

"That would be lovely," Erikah said. "Wine is perfect for a hot day like this one."

Paco stepped to the side and ushered the couple into his home. They walked in, as if the place was familiar to them. Their steps carried no hesitancy.

"I don't trust them, Guardián," Humo said. "Haven't you read of all the awful things they have done?"

"Have I read them?" Paco asked, insulted by the audacity. "Yes, I read them. I read them to <u>you</u> because <u>you</u> are an illiterate."

"Now you're just being hurtful!"

Paco bent down and grabbed Humo by the back of the neck. "I need you to relax. Everything is okay."

Humo sighed. "Okay. I trust you, Guardián."

###

The three sat around the table while Paco refilled two dwindling glasses of port wine. The couple had many questions for Paco, who was intrigued by their presence in a country whose government, while neutral for most of the war, ultimately ended up siding with the Allies. Benno drank his wine with haste, while Paco sipped his. Erikah declined a glass, despite her saying outside, moments ago, that wine would be perfect for a hot day.

Erikah had picked up Paco's shirt off the floor and handed it to him right when he walked inside. She had already placed their duffel bag beside the front door. Paco slipped the shirt on and fastened the buttons from the top down after he had sat down. Benno's suit jacket hung on the back of his chair, revealing a holstered pistol under his armpit.

"So, mister and misses Schmitz... what makes you think I would know your son, Ernst?"

Before he had even asked this first question, Benno was already halfway finished with his second glass of wine.

"Have you heard of the name Hugo Sperrle?"

"Of course. He was... how do you say it in Germany? A generalfeldmarschall?" Paco asked, butchering the pronunciation.

"And what else do you know of this man?" Benno asked.

Paco peered over at Humo, who was sitting in front of the couch, watching them intensely. His ears were up and his rear was off the floor, ready to spring into action if needed. He mirrored the demeanor his guardian was able to keep hidden from the guests.

"I am ignorant in my knowledge of German army officials," Paco admitted.

"We had a son serve under him in the Great War when Hugo was a Hauptamann... how do you say that in Spanish? Captain, I believe?"

Paco nodded, even though he was not sure if that was true or not. "Was this Ernst who had fought in this war?"

"No," Erikah said. "We had three sons. Walter served in the Great War."

"I owned a factory that did decently," Benno interrupted. "My family had always been loyal to the empire and the war efforts." He paused to finish his wine in one gulp. He held out his glass and Paco refilled. Benno continued as the purple wine splashed in the glass. "When his plane was shot down by the British, it devastated us. They told us it would be best not to look at our son's corpse for it had been so mangled and burned from the crash."

Humo rested his rear on the wood floor. He sensed Paco's anxiety wither as his sympathy began to bloom. Humo's ears rested down as he leaned backwards against the cushions.

"Times were hard after that. Not just for us but for the country," Erikah said. "It seemed like we were losing money every day. At times we had to forgo meals. That is the only reason why we did not protest when Ernst joined the military. There was an opportunity to build a career during his service and we supported him."

"And Ernst, he fought in Spain?" Paco asked.

"Let me ask you a question," Benno said.

Paco did not even see Benno finish his glass of port wine. He held it out again, in the same manner as a rude customer who hurries the waiter. Paco filled the glass again with the last drops from the bottle. The purple had stained Benno's lips and teeth, making it appear as if he had smudged lipstick.

"Why did you choose to fight for Franco?"

While Paco never received this question before, he already knew the answer. "My parents were monarchists who hated Moroccans. Despite myself never having a sentimental connection to royal traditions, I have always been a strict Catholic. Friends of mine who advocated for Franco showed me snippets of what the anarchists and communists read. I did not like what Marx had to say about religion. I felt that I had to defend the Church."

Benno slurped the wine down as if it were a race. The drink dripped down the side of his mouth and fell off his chin as if he was spilling dark tears. Paco stood up to fetch another bottle from his cabinet. As he uncorked the bottle, he heard Erikah's voice from behind him.

"Do you feel you did right by your faith?"

"I will be forgiven, regardless," Paco said, as if he had rehearsed the response.

Paco turned around to see the couple staring at him. Humo was watching them, once again on guard as Paco's body tensed. He poured himself a glass before serving Benno. Benno continued with his retelling.

"Ernst served under Hugo just like his older brother. The Republicans shot him down over Madrid. Unlike Walter, our forces were not able to recover his body to properly lay him to rest."

Paco took out another cigarette when his extinguished. Benno's coat hung over the back of his chair, so Erikah reached into the pocket and pulled out the same lighter as before. She lit a cigarette for Paco and took one out of her purse.

"You are a Catholic," Benno said. "You believe in the holy trinity. Our youngest boy, Otto, served in this last war."

"I believe I identified the pattern in this story," Paco said. "My condolences for your boys. All three of them."

###

They drank awhile longer. Paco had stopped, now feeling the effects of intoxication. Benno's face sagged as his mouth dangled open and his eyes became incapable of focusing. Erikah, who had begun to drink conservatively, sat and smoked her cigarette between her sips. She stood up at one point to sit on the couch beside Humo. Humo protested, until Paco told him to cease. Erikah stroked his chin until Humo's tail began to wag.

"I am sorry to say, but I never met Ernst."

"He was a tall, handsome boy," Erikah said. "Brawny, too. Black hair, just like yours."

"I am sorry," Paco said. "Our paths never crossed."

Benno stood up and the chair legs scratched the wood as it slid back. His inebriation almost made him lose balance and collapse.

"The damn Hugo owes me three sons!" he shouted in Spanish. He continued to yell, but Paco could not translate his German, but recognized the word wrath. Benno took a breath and looked over, appearing to gather his composure. "I need to relieve myself," he said, as he nearly stumbled outside.

Humo's tail still wagged, as Erikah stroked under his chin. "I might have been too hard on these people," the dog said. "Too quick to judge. I hardly ever do that."

"I apologize for my husband. We were just hoping to learn more about Ernst before we make the final journey to South America," Erikah explained before pouring the wine down her throat. "We have no other family left alive. It is just us."

Paco walked over and sat beside her. Humo jumped off the couch and sat beside his feet.

"Do you believe wonderful things can be born from grief?" she asked.

"I believe that is where all wonderful things are born."

She put her hand on her stomach. "My grief is cradling life in my womb, right as we speak."

Paco was shocked. She appeared too old to conceive. While he had been drinking, he was not rude enough to question the matter.

"It is still early," she said. "But I know it will be another boy. A son I will not let die fighting anyone's war."

She finished her glass of wine. The color swirled with her dark shade of red lipstick.

"You should check on Benno," she said. "He is very drunk and could wander away." She slunk into the cushions with a grin plastered across her face. "I am a lightweight," she admitted. "I feel very woozy."

Erikah's eyes closed. Paco got up and began to walk to the door. When he passed his trunk, Humo protested.

"Bring your gun!" he shouted. "Who knows what he's capable of."

"I thought you said you were quick to judge them?"

"I don't remember saying that."

Paco opened his trunk and took the pistol resting on top of his old army uniform. Erikah was nearly asleep and did not notice Paco hook the holster around his waist or hear the cocking of the pistol.

Outside, he saw that the evening was approaching. Humo followed Paco, walking beside him with such subordination. They stepped around back to find their guest. At the rear of his cottage, he found Benno sitting on a stool behind Alfonso.

"What are you doing out here?" Paco asked.

"Just admiring your steed," the German slurred. He held his palms out towards Paco. "Der hoden," he said. "Enormous!"

"Look! Look! Look!" Humo yelled.

"What's gotten into you?" asked Paco.

"That damn bird is here!" he shouted.

Stationed on a nearby rock, they spotted the Egyptian vulture. Its orange beak and the feathers that looked like needles on its neck made it stand out.

"I told you I saw it!" Humo yelled.

Benno said something in German that Paco could not translate. Benno took out his pistol and took aim at the bird to shoot.

"No! Wait!" Paco tried to warn.

Benno discharged the weapon. The echo from the blast boomed throughout the valley. His shot missed and the bird flew away as Humo continued to yell. The commotion frightened Alfonso, who bucked and kicked out his back hooves. The horseshoe collided against Benno's temple and Paco saw blood splatter as he witnessed the horrific sight.

"Oh my god!" Humo shouted. "Did you see that?" He ran over to the body.

Paco crept towards Benno, whose head bled out onto the dirt as he was sprawled on his back. There was no movement.

Humo began sniffing the wound and the ground around him. "Disgusting. There's chunks of his brain around."

"Humo, get away."

"Yuck! It tastes awful."

"Why are you licking it?"

The commotion died down. Humo was no longer barking, Alfonso stopped bucking, and Benno had no more words to slur.

"You shot my husband."

Paco turned around and saw Erikah standing before them, with a pistol in her hand that he had not seen before. From the sight of the scene, her accusation was not misplaced. But Paco was afraid he would not have the time to explain.

"Erikah, please," he said, reciting her name gently; attempting to sound familiar to her.

She took aim and pulled the trigger. Humo yelled, "Guardián, look out!" before jumping in front of Paco. Humo whimpered as he fell to the ground. Paco gasped in horror. Without thinking, Paco drew his weapon and took aim. His lone shot hit Erikah in the forehead and she collapsed backwards like a fallen structure.

"Great shot, Guardián," Humo said, now standing between the corpse and Paco.

"I thought she shot you!"

"No. I think she missed us both."

"Then why were you whimpering like she hit you?"

"It was so loud... I was scared."

Together, they both crept over towards the body. The scene terrified Paco, not able to believe what he had just done.

Humo sniffed the corpse and the ground around her where the soil soaked up the blood.

"I can smell her brains on the ground," Humo said. "Yuck, they taste just like his!"

A couple hours passed, and no authorities came to the isolated area of the valley. Paco knew they were likely not going to arrive, but he wanted an opportunity to explain in case anyone who heard the gunfire decided to come and investigate. The land around him remained silent. The vultures and bugs would gather soon, and he did not want his home to resemble the battlefields he had seen during his years fighting.

He put on his army boots that he kept in the trunk and placed the couple in the wagon he kept and rolled them towards the thick patches of trees that made up miniature forests. As he rolled them through the dirt, he tried not to look down at their disfigured heads. The sight repulsed him.

Surrounded by the trees, Paco began to dig with a gaslight beside him. He dug two holes beside each other near a tree that distinguished itself from the others. The formation of the branches resembled a cross, which he felt was an appropriate marker for the grave site.

He spent his hours and sweat digging two six-foot graves. When he finished, he hoisted the bodies up one at a time and dropped them in. With his eyes shut, and his head turned away, he positioned them with their arms crossed. With both of them in their respective graves, he began to cover them in dirt.

With the graves filled, he recited a prayer. He kept it short and made the sign of the cross when he finished. After he kissed his knuckle, he took the wagon and headed back to his cottage.

Paco parked the wagon beside Alfonso. He walked past the drying blood in the ground that was still visible. Though, already, it was becoming a vestige.

Humo was waiting by the door when Paco stepped inside. He jumped up and began wagging his rear, thrilled to see his friend again. Humo sniffed the dirt that covered the boots.

Benno's jacket was still hanging on the back of the chair. Finished glasses and hollowed bottles of wine littered the cottage. Their duffel bag was by the door, unopened, likely containing all of their possessions from Berlin.

Paco collapsed on the couch after slipping off his boots. Humo pounced beside him, sitting upright as if he was imitating a human.

"She was pregnant," Paco muttered. "I murdered a pregnant woman."

"They are the ones who came in here and caused trouble. I never trusted either of them, anyway."

"They came to learn more about their son and now they're dead. All because of me."

"Don't feel too bad for them. The man couldn't even kill that vile vulture!" Humo yelled.

Paco took a cigarette out from his pocket. His hands trembled as he slipped the smoke out from the pack. He saw the couple's lighter, and the symbol engraved that had become synonymous with sinister men.

Paco thought of all the newspapers he had read during the last war. The headlines that called attention to death, destruction, and genocide. He focused on those words and used the headlines he could recall as a mechanism to control his breathing.

"They owned a factory," Paco said. "And she was pregnant. I killed a pregnant woman. I never killed a pregnant woman before."

"Well, that you know of," Humo said. "God only knows the people that got killed by those bombs you dropped."

Humo spoke with such innocence, as if he had meant for his comment to be comforting. The words Paco heard only made him cry. He wept as the skin on his face and palms became damp. When he relieved his palms from his face, Humo leaned forward to sniff the tears before licking them.

It was now dark outside. Humo looked out the window as if he had not noticed before.

"If you want my opinion," the dog said. "I think this was a peculiar day."

Paco let out an abrupt, solitary laugh. Saliva spit out from his mouth and landed on his knee. When Humo went to sniff the saliva, Paco began to massage his ear. Humo collapsed into his guardian's lap.

"Today, you saw firsthand that I am a wicked man," Paco said. "I always said that god will forgive me, but I don't know. How could he? Why should he?"

"That does not make sense, Guardián," Humo said earnestly, while still resting on Paco's lap. "I love you. So how could you be a bad person? It's illogical."

Despite the depression, Paco smiled even though his stomach was in knots and the heaviness he felt paralyzed him. Still, he began to pet Humo. His hands ran through the curly hairs that reminded him of springboards. It was so quiet through the cottage, that their heavy breathing was all Paco could hear. Humo stretched, letting out a grunt. He rolled over on his back and let out a deep sigh.

"Rub my belly, please," he requested.

Paco obliged.

3 Ailments

I'm incredibly ill. I think. Apparently, you can inherit family trauma. If that is true, what else can we inherit? Is that what preexisting conditions are? That might just be an insurance thing, but I'm not sure.

I need a doctor. I feel like hell and I know my mind is breaking down. There is something wrong. There's a list in my pocket of my three ailments that I hope the doctor can help me with. He has a white mustache and a Tufts medical degree framed on the wall. So far, he seems nice enough.

Good thing I memorized the list because the paper is in my pants' pocket and I had to take them off for the initial exam. He asks me what seems to be the problem today. I tell him there are three concerns I have and he makes the helpful suggestion of starting with the first one.

"I might be an alcoholic," I say. Not much of a proclamation. It does not feel liberating or healing.

His next question seems reasonable. How many drinks do I have a night? I tell him I am not sure, but I have at least one glass of wine or a beer with dinner. His next question is silly. He asks if I've tried to quit, and I tell him why would I quit if I am not sure I'm an alcoholic. Maybe he needs more context, so I explain that my brother and grandfather were both alcoholics. My grandfather drank so much that he died during a drunken stupor when he fell down a flight of stairs and cracked open the back of his head.

He suggests I see a therapist or a social worker to delve deeper. I request he draw blood or run x-rays to determine if I am addicted to alcohol and to what extent.

For some reason that is not possible. How can there be no tests that can tell if and how much someone may be addicted to something? They have tests to see if someone has diabetes or cancer. They can even tell you what type of diabetes you have or how much cancer is in your body.

Apparently the medical technology does not exist. The doctor's only advice, other than talking to a mental health professional, is to try and cut back on drinking and see how that goes.

We move on and go into the second ailment.

"I forgot how to speak Spanish."

The doctor is acting like he does not understand so I repeat myself. To clarify, he asks if I ever knew Spanish and I tell him only a few words and phrases, but my grandmother did. She spoke Spanish her whole life. If trauma can be inherited, why not language? All history lives in the brain.

Grandma used to speak Spanish to my mother and even me. She was born in Buffalo and lived in Brooklyn for many years but grew up in Spanish-speaking households. Her parents were from Ronda, Spain, and spoke with that famous lisp. I demonstrate the lisp to the doctor with one of the few phrases I know but that doesn't seem to help his confusion.

I go on and tell him that she had nicknames for me in Spanish. She used to call me, "mi chico de ojos azules." I get emotional sharing that memory with the physician and he does not seem to understand that I need his diagnosis. So I ask him again:

"Why can't I speak Spanish?"

He seems frazzled. Maybe I went to the wrong doctor. He tells me if I never actually learned to speak the language, then I never forgot. It's odd that I have to explain to him the recent study about how we can inherit our family's trauma. He begins to lecture me but my confidence is fading.

This was my mistake. I should have gone to a neurologist. I ask for a recommendation, but he says any neurologist will tell me the same thing. I'm getting ready to leave and he asks what is my last issue. Even though I have lost faith, I share with him.

"I can't get an erection."

He asks how long this has been going on. I tell him for about thirteen hours, but I think he hears me say "days" instead. I describe my girlfriend to him and how wonderful our relationship has been lately. We've been having sex all the time and she drives me wild.

I tell the doctor about how excited she makes me. That she'll often sit naked on the edge of the bed with her legs spread and her toes pressed down against the floor on the balls of her feet to steady herself. She'll then take her finger and graze the tip from the bottom of her pussy all the way up to her clit and stroke it gently clockwise. She has me massage her breasts as she breathes into my ear and her breath tickles my entire body and makes my bones shiver. She does this until I can't contain myself and drop to my knees and begin licking where she was massaging. Her moans make me so hard and when she grabs my hair I lose all control and I love the way she tastes so much that sometimes I'll just cum right there before her. The cum sticks to my thigh hair and I try to catch my breath while I keep licking her at the same time until she cums too and my mouth and chin are drenched with her.

The doctor seems interested in the story, but I can't tell if he is taking notes or not. I hope he is following this because I need his help. I know for a fact that my parents stopped having sex the last twenty or so years of their life and I would kill myself if I inherited whatever condition inflicted that upon them.

Surprisingly, the doctor begins scribbling on a pad and hands me a prescription. He says this should help with erectile dysfunction.

"That's it?" I ask.

He just nods and recommends I see a therapist for the other issues I disclosed to him today. He also suggests I try not drinking to see if that helps with my erections. I think I'll try the medication first.

*****

Picking up the pills at the pharmacy is easy enough. Although, the pills aren't covered by insurance, so swiping my credit card hurts. At least pharmacists don't ask intruding questions. You just pay and be on your way. I remember trying to get cough medicine in Austria. I wasn't sick, but I needed it for my jet lag to get to sleep. The pharmacist kept asking me questions regarding my symptoms and it's not like I could tell them it was for recreation.

I know he was just trying to help, but I didn't want to explain everything. This doctor, here in the States, wasn't so great but hopefully he'll help me get a boner again. And maybe this medicine will help me remember Spanish the next time I cum.

Fingers crossed.

The high E

At 39 years old, his dreams have come true. He is on stage performing alongside his bandmates to an enthusiastic crowd. There is a woman with a shaved head near the front row. They exchange glances and his callused fingers create a psychedelic melody that conjures the rare confidence for him to give her a wink. She smiles back and bites her purple painted lips after taking a sip from her foam-filled cup.

The song they are performing was inspired by a period that surprised the 32-year-old lead singer while she was on ecstasy and watching "I Married a Strange Person." This song, conceived from menstruation, is titled after the animated film.

With his pinky, he presses down on the high E. The thinnest, steel string plucks like a razor wire and severs the top of his finger. Half of the nail is gone, only leaving the nail bed and gushing crimson that is sprouting like a fountain with faulty pipes. No one in the crowd notices. They continue to groove and the band plays on, including the maimed guitarist who is now in agony.

Thank god there is no encore. He wraps a bandana around his wound and goes searching for his amputated finger in the hopes it can be sewn back on. The dive bar venue is clearing out and the now dim lit lights put on display all the empty cups and bottles and puddles of spilled drinks soaking up litter that never reached the trashcan.

"Excuse me," he says to the bartender closing out the last tab. "Have you seen a piece of my finger? It flew off stage while I was playing."

"Sorry, no. Check the manager's office and see if it made it to the lost & found."

The guitarist raps on the wooden, warped door in the back with the poster of last month's run of shows hanging on by the last bit of strength remaining in the adhesive of the scotch tape.

"Good show tonight," the manager says, punching numbers into his calculator.

"Thank you. By chance did anyone turn in a piece of a finger?

The manager recommends he check the bin, but there are only phones, coats, and a purse. The guitarist broaches members of the audience who linger, but none of them have seen the missing piece of his mutilation.

He stands outside in the frigid night. He sees the faint stain spreading in the dark fabric of his wrapped bandana. With a sigh, he surrenders the effort. He fastens the guitar strap and walks towards the bus stop.

"Excuse me," he hears along with footsteps.

Turning around, he recognizes the shaved head and the purple smile from the show. Her hurried steps slow down and she stands eye level to him. In the cup of her palm, wrapped in a tissue so soiled that the color turned brown, is his missing finger piece.

"I was waiting for you outside to give this back." She offers the finger as if it is a delicate gift and he accepts it as if being offered to hold a stranger's newborn. He unravels the tissue and sees the top of his pinky which makes him smile.

"Thank you," he says to her, looking into her soft irises. Even though his fingers and soul are not occupied with creating melody, a slither of confidence from earlier endures. "Do you maybe want to grab a late night coffee around the corner?" he asks.

She nods. "That sounds great."

"I'm sorry. Is that too forward?"

The woman shakes her head and they begin to walk together. He folds the tissue around the finger again and puts it in his pocket next to cough drop wrappers. As they walk, she looks down at his makeshift bandaged hand.

"Do you instead want to grab a cup of coffee at the ER?" she suggests.

He shakes his head. "I don't have insurance. I'll put it in ice until I can think of an idea."

The pair turn a corner and continue their small talk. Illuminating letters of the cafe appear at the end of the block. Inside at the table, they sip coffee together while his fingertip lays in a cup of ice.

Changes
or
(Antonio Sánchez Saves the Day)

1:19am

This fish slivers through the vessels of the body as if the bloodstreams were dormant canals.

I settled with drums as my passion. I wanted to be a singer who could render devotion through chords better than anyone else. Half my childhood was choir practice. But after listening to Charles Bradley sing "God Bless America," I had to ask myself, why even fucking bother?

So I drum. I'm a drummer. A glorified metronome who, at best, can guise itself with rhythm and funk.

Self-deprecation is an evolutionary trait my family developed. That and alcoholism. I've always had to be a little different by tiptoeing over boundaries, especially the ones I inherited. A contrarian through and through and there's enough booze in me already. That's why I'm sitting on the hood of my Honda, in front of abandoned freight train tracks that look like some Post-Soviet Belarusian oblast, sipping on cough syrup like it's dry whiskey from a flask.

There's a spliff in my shirt pocket and I'm going to light it with my uncle's zippo that he took off a dead Vietnamese. I may play in a soul singer's band but tonight I feel pretty grunge. The 90s ensnared a part of me. That decade maimed my foot in a bear trap and I never gnawed off the mangled limb, so I just drag the contraption wherever I go. The rest of me matured but I went down so many different paths I don't think the components of myself ever reunited.

I'm near the bottom of my plastic, purple, pharmacy flask. A car's high beams pass behind me and for a second a cargo hold looks like it has the nuclear symbol painted over the rusted metal. My lungs suck down the burning dope and instead of being paranoid of boys in blue I'm now worried about the KGB, a different kind of thug from an empire that's long dead.

Cough syrup and marijuana is a mystical combination. I once conjured a ghost with this formula like a Slavic pagan séance. What spirits are waiting to be summoned from under these decaying tracks?

Last year I was at a hotel down in Natchez. I indulged in my mixture and a woman stood at the foot of the bed. She dressed like a 19ᵗʰ century call girl and so I asked her what she was doing here. She told me, "I have a habit of visiting potential johns." I asked if she wanted to fuck and she laughed. "Soliciting is just a habit. I told you," she repeated. "Even if we wanted to, it's not compatible with you on that side."

She continued to speak in that colonial hotel with the Mississippi River right outside. "This visit doesn't have to be for naught. I can share something about your past or future." I asked if she could really see in the future. This time she didn't laugh. Her lips grew brighter and her eyes ignited in a smoky texture. "Time doesn't work like that here. Events are just places you can see, not moments that have or haven't happened." Who doesn't want their future told to them? So I asked what will happen to me later in life. A vague question earned a vague response. "You'll be known for sharing wicked stories of men with rotted hearts." I asked for more. "I cannot say. I'm not even allowed to be here. We're not supposed to visit the inebriated. And you still owe me for what I already shared." I asked what I owed and she laughed again. This time she curtsied with her frilly skirt. "You'll compensate me in the astral plane. I've already seen you do so." Are you going to hypnotize me, I asked for some reason. "Only those who want to be hypnotized can be. Otherwise it's a hollow influence."

I blinked and she left.

Weed is burning and the thick, artificial taste of NyQuil is still lounging in my throat. Despite enduring my discomfort, my ritual fails to summon any spirits. Empty cargo holds surround me. She told me they are not supposed to visit a person in this state, but maybe another one, like her, will break the rules. I'm counting on it.

After all, I've never seen anyone from the other side while sober.

I can't drive. I can drive, just not at this moment. I crawl into the backseat. It's cold in the car but my body doesn't care. At first, I keep opening my eyes, expecting to see a long-deceased soul staring outside through the window at me. I'm expecting it so much that the absence startles me. My eyelids don't just shut for the night, they practically die and anchor themselves down.

7:49am

Gluttony makes this fish ill. It nestles in the stomach with its own protruding belly pushing against the gut.

I'm not an easy sight this morning. The rush hour congestion behind me isn't doing any favors. I open the door and step outside to puke. I crawl back inside the car to lay down and squint at my phone through a litany of unanswered messages.

Rehearsal is later in the evening. Some of the texts are reminders from the band that they wrote in a "this is the last straw" sort-of tone. I have one from my sister which I delete before reading, not because I'm angry at her but because I don't feel like reading what I know she's going to say. One of my apps pushes a notification of movie times. *"Birdman or (The*

Unexpected Virtue of Ignorance)" is playing just a few exits down at the same time as *Gone Girl* and that new Keanu Reeves action movie.

My breath is rancid.

My eyes close again, but the jammed highway makes for the worst lullaby. Somehow, even though it's the morning, the sound is haunting. Any one of those blasting horns could be coming from a god-damn psychopath directing their frustration at some sociopath who will become a random person's problem later today. It's noisy and I'm thinking about all of this.

I fall asleep anyway.

11:11am

After digestion, this fish plunges up to the neuro system to find shelter. This is where it was born.

I see the time on my phone and mumble to myself "make a wish." I always say that, but I never actually make one. My stomach purrs so I guess my wish is to get something to eat.

The highway is empty again. No more broken heroes on a last chance power drive (my parents should be proud I keep the classics in my heart). It's an easy merge into the lane and I drive ahead leaving behind that nuclear-esque dystopia.

There's a diner just three minutes away. It's a chain with underpaid employees who never give a shit that people park their cars in the lot to shoot and snort scag. Why would the employees care? At least they know those people won't create commotion, unlike the booze hounds they have to deal with on their shift. Cops patrol the lot though because of course they do. Their budget is too big and they have military grade weapons. No one who has ever held a machine that can reign death upon a population has ever once said "let's just idle and take in the pleasant weather. Maybe that kind old lady on the stoop can tell us about her apple pie recipes." The potential for obliteration can inspire a lot but it sure does not inspire idleness. So you'll see them more here at night, knocking on windows, pulling people out who can barely stand while they slap cold metal cuffs around their wrists.

Oinking while dragging them to the paddy-wagon.

The waitress is nice. I've sat in her section before. Not often enough to initiate familiar small talk, but just enough for awkwardness and hesitancy. I'm sure she recognizes my sleeve. My arm resembles an arbor with all the wrapping, tattooed green vines. I look around and don't see anyone who was working here when I had a late dinner last night.

The whole purpose of these kinds of retro diners is to spark nostalgia. It's a bit misleading if you ask me. There's no way they'll let you smoke and everyone besides me is wearing sweatpants and some kind of graphic shirt with whichever superhero hit it big at the box office. Somehow in just jeans, a silver shirt, and some sneakers I'm the one overdressed. Other than the 60s music and the unregulated cholesterol count, nothing here is nostalgic.

That reminds me to check my notifications again. There are those movie showings I can catch if I eat fast enough. I drink enough coffee to caffeinate a comatose Sasquatch. I still feel exhausted, and I know all of these drinks are going to make me piss like a busted pipe full of jet fuel, but I'm not making it through the day without it.

I'm tapping my finger and counting in 16th notes. Grooves sound better in 16th notes when playing a standard 4/4, in my opinion. The crisp hi hat taps clustered between the bass drum and the snare throughout the measure have a mesmeric influence. I'm brainstorming a simple groove to get

through a new song in practice later. The lyrics and melody
are escaping me, but I think keeping the groove simple and
playing an accent note on the snare of 4 and ghost notes on the
'e' and 'uh" of 4 will accompany the song nicely.

I rehearse with my fingers and feet right there on the
table.

It's only a 20-minute drive to the theater. Parking is
easy enough and I just pull right into a spot. I decide to return
a text to ease the singer's anxiety about me not showing up
this evening. As I tap the screen I search in my backpack and
grab my flask. At the same time I notice a message in my spam
about the MFA writing program at my alma mater Sarah
Lawrence.

The theater's near empty and I get a text back from our
singer with just the letter 'k.' This comes off as passive
aggressive. I know it's in my head the same way the clerk's
shitty attitude as I order my one ticket is just in my head.

I'm halfway down the stained carpeted corridor
looking for theater 17. I take out my flask and I swear to god I
don't remember polishing off all the whiskey yesterday.
There's not enough time to drive over to the liquor store
before the trailers end. If the movie blows, I'll just bail. I
should probably do that anyway. Why sit through a movie I'm
not enjoying just because I bought the ticket? I'm flipping the
paper stub between my fingers. 17 is right ahead.

The lettering for "Birdman" illuminates red.

4:37pm

*Despite this fish being home, it is restless. It has desires to devour
but has lost ounces of power.*

I can't shut up about the movie. Everyone else in the band has already seen it and adored the soundtrack. The band wants to focus on the new song we're trying to put together and I just want to talk Birdman. They've been telling me to go see it before the theaters pull it for new releases. Seems like a sin to pull a film like that. I can only imagine what blockbuster piece of shit is going to get swapped in.

Birdman's plot was good, but Antonio Sánchez was the star. A whole performance of drum solos is a feat to behold. Anyone left unimpressed does not know a god-damn thing about drums. I had to piss during the whole movie, but I held it in trying to decipher how he could have been playing those beats. I'm still baffled and pretty sure my bladder has now endured irreversible damage. We're literally practicing our newest song right fucking now and we have to stop because I'm as far off tempo that's acceptable for a drummer.

They're all holding their instruments. Their guitars and basses and brasses. The piano keeps tapping the keys because he is feeling the rhythm. Everyone seems annoyed but not in the same way they have been with me. More like a "will you just fucking focus, please" kind of way. So I try to recenter myself and focus while also noticing I'm sweating more than normal. I forgot to stop off at the liquor store before coming over here.

I try and recenter myself again.

I play the groove I practiced at the diner earlier.

I decide to add another ghost note on the "&" of 2. I like how it sounds and the bassist seems to jive with it.

This song that is being birthed right now has me captivated. I'm hearing all the keys and chords amalgamate. Our singer bursts out keys and the instrumentals make their respected changes. I start to play quarter notes. Even though that wasn't planned or discussed the decision somehow conjoins all the sounds into a perfect, polygamous union.

We continue to play and I can hear the ghost I met a year ago. She's not here with us but her voice is more vivid than it has been in my memories. I'm allowed visitors on the other side in this state. At least I assume. I don't see why that wouldn't be allowed.

The music has me entranced even though I can't hear one instrument or one voice any more clearly than another.

Maybe I need to rest. Maybe I need to take time to explore this hypnotism. I have the joy of finishing this song, and, when we are done, I'm excited to go back and play the others we crafted together.

11:14am

The fish lingers and broods, whispering to itself in the hopes that the door to his own home will open again.

If only I woke up three minutes earlier. I just missed a chance for another wish. I can use a few more wishes. Who in this world, or the next, can't find purpose for a few more wishes?

Right after rehearsal a couple weeks ago I scavenged all the serums and potions tucked away and forgotten in the dark corners of my medicine cabinet. Thank god for my sister who knocked on my door and discovered her brother on the floor spooning with an empty bottle of Jack. I'm blessed she came by and drove me to the ER, but, still, detox was a bitch.

I just wanted to go home that night and play my drums.

There's nothing cinematic about the shaking and puking and weight loss, no matter how much you look like a Jared Leto douche bag. The worst is when you're forced to smell your own diarrhea because it's a dead heat between shitting and puking and you can't flush because you don't want any brown or green saturation to splash back to your face. They don't show you that conundrum in the art house dramas and Hollywood passion projects. There's no Oscar nomination or standing ovation waiting outside the bathroom.

It's difficult sitting here, in this room, in this building, for too many reasons. I keep thinking of the song our band created, but I know I am only recollecting a memory of that sound. My memory can't replicate those notes. Not exactly. Our brains don't keep souvenirs. Instead they give abstract sculptures while convincing us it's realism.

Typhoons of shame and self-inflicted depravity hit me. I have no defenses. Though, I am blessed for the tremors of relief that occasionally rock me. I don't recall ever experiencing delight in bursts.

There is a man sitting at the chair beside my bed when I step out of the bathroom. I assume he is here for my therapy session. Today is my first one-on-one. At first he reminds me of James Brown and gives me a warm smile. I sit cross-legged on the mattress.

"How are you feeling?" he asks me. His tone has a kindness that seems foreign with clinical dialogue. I tell him today, like most, is a rough day. He speaks with a subtle lisp and tells me he understands, and shares "I've felt like an empty shell." He goes on and tells me about his mother and how much he suffered when she was taking her last breaths followed by a last goodbye. When describing her illness, he uses the word crisis. I've never heard anyone use that word to describe someone who is sick. I'm not really looking at him while he is talking. This might be rude, but I haven't been able to look anyone in the eye since I started rehabilitation. It's been hard to listen to anyone, but every word he says is clear to me. He continues like he knows with unwavering confidence that I am listening. He says he knows I'm an artist and he says artist instead of drummer or musician. This makes him sound less and less like a therapist. I ask if he plays music and he tells me he still does because music is eternal no matter which side of the universe you are on. "A real good artist learns to be a better person through all the changes they've been through." My eyelids are shut but translucent. The light doesn't seem to be coming from a particular source. The flashes of purple are manifesting from my own tension with the anchors I have yet to detach from my eyes. I finally look up at him but he's not there anymore.

I feel like my mind is coming down from an elevated consciousness or even just a regular high, but instead of a free-fall collision it's a gentle glide.

I look around the room. The carpet and desk and mattress that have remained the same for the past week appear undiscovered as if I've never been here before. As if I stepped out from a void.

The door opens and a nurse walks in to tell me I'm late for my therapy appointment. I tell her there was just someone here. She says all sessions are in the office and that therapists are not allowed to meet patients in their room.

??:??

This fish is mostly in a state of retrograde but dreams of escaping a stalled remission.

_____ Simon

His wife is going to try and leave him. He does not know this for sure. Certainty can never be a hundred percent, but in this instance he is correct.

Poor Simon.

How is he supposed to understand an immigrant's experience? His own family has put in immeasurable effort to assimilate. Because of their investment, their native language is erased from their lineage and the cuisine is now Bennigans and shopping mall food courts.

His wife misses Minsk. There is nothing about America that reminds her of her homeland. She feels a hollowness familiar to him, but yet completely incomprehensible.

Misguided Simon.

Everyone told him being a real estate agent is easy money, especially in this market. No one told him about the 80-20 rule. Around eighty percent of home sales go to twenty percent of agents.

He needs to sell this house. That's the only way he can keep his wife from leaving him. His fate lies in the hands of getting this one disregarded home off the market.

Desperate Simon.

He tries to straighten the "For Sale" sign planted in the lawn. That is the real problem, he tells himself. It has nothing to do with the black bear that lives on the roof of the house.

It's a remote property, full of character and surrounded by lush hills. The garden in the back is full of gladiolus flowers in perpetual bloom. The lateral white wood leads the eye up to the most gorgeous Wallaba shingles that have gone undamaged despite a full-grown black bear walking all over them.

Nervous Simon.

His client's car pulls into the driveway. She is a television actress whom Simon has never heard of. She only does commercials. He does not understand how a single woman who occasionally acts in commercials can afford to live on her own. The royalties pay well, apparently. Who knew?

She dresses as if she is a Hollywood golden age star. She even has the polka dot head scarf and sunglasses. This is her ninth property walkthrough with Simon and quite possibly the last. He approaches to shake her hand and showcase that salesman smile he taught himself.

"Ms. Desmond, good morning. I'm looking forward to showing you this property."

"It has lovely curb appeal," she says.

The black bear is on the other side of the roof and out of their sight. Simon leads her to the front door and begins the tour. The home, with its isolation, has a cottage aesthetic but with modern amenities. There is a chandelier in the dining room and built in maple bookcases in the guestroom. The display furniture conjures the image of children playing quietly and a father walking through the front door after a workday.

"What do you think so far, Ms. Desmond?" he asks.

"You say there is also a garden?"

"There is, with trimmed hedges and flowers that don't need tending. A perfect patio for your romance novels and cocktails."

"I'm excited to see it."

Optimistic Simon.

He leads her to the patio and the garden is magical. The flowers are alive and thriving. Flowers that don't need a green thumb to care for them is a remarkable selling point.

They take a seat on the patio furniture. He wants her to envision a fantasy of what every day could be. The black bear is still out of sight, and he assumes it rolled over to the other side of the roof because the black bear loves to roll on his back.

Fidgety Simon.

She is going to ask what the catch is. The sellers are asking way below the market value for similar homes in the county. That is suspicious for a buyer.

He knows she is going to ask if the home has a faulty structure or shoddy repairs (it doesn't). She'll ask if there is crime nearby (there is none). There is no way she is going to ask if a bear is living on the roof (there is) so he will have to come clean.

Motivated Simon.

He is going to sell her this property, damn it. She loves this home and he knows that. There is only one more hurdle and his marriage is saved and he can afford to provide a nuclear lifestyle for his wife.

Unlike past showings to former clients, he has his talking points ready. He knows what to say and what not to say. Since this is his last chance, he knows he may have to tread in a gray area where honesty is not entirely absent but deception oversees the domain.

Prepared Simon.

"Okay, so I give. What is the drawback?"

"Well," he begins. "You see, the seller inherited this property from their grandmother, a twenty-year widow. They have been having difficulty selling the place because most buyers cannot get past one . . . blunt . . . detail."

"And what is the blunt detail?"

At that moment, as if on cue, the black bear crawls into view. The black bear sits down and begins scratching his belly with long claws. Ms. Desmond raises her manicured eyebrows. Before she can inquire, Simon begins the partial disclosure.

"You see, this black bear comes with the home."

"Comes with the home? What are you talking about? Isn't there someone you can call to get rid of it?"

"I'm afraid not. The county has gotten it off the roof a few times and took it into custody. Yet, the bear always escapes and ends up back on the roof exactly three weeks later. There is no explaining the phenomenon. When they first built the house back in 1888, the daughter left a jar of honey outside her window. Since then the bear has stayed."

Ms. Desmond stares at the black bear, who is now rolled over on his back to soak in the sun while he naps. She is perplexed and who can blame her. She proceeds to ask a reasonable question.

"I imagine it makes a lot of noise, no?"

"Oddly enough, no." Simon is going to stick to his practiced talking points. "You can't hear the bear from inside. He was on the roof the whole time while we were inside. It is silent, as if his paws are made of feathers. And he has never crawled down, so you and your future family will never be in danger. Unless you are looking at him, like now, it will be as if he is not even there."

He leaves out the fact that the black bear will sometimes hang from the gutters, swaying back and forth. The black bear only does this, from what anyone can tell, as a way to play some kind of silly game. Still, the gutters somehow won't break (a testament to the construction). This would be another selling point he would use if asked, but he keeps quiet for now.

She thinks for a moment.

"Doesn't it need to hibernate?"

Simon shakes his head. He is not entirely sure, but he sticks with what he rehearsed.

"So the bear is completely silent? No noise at all?"

This is the question Simon prepped the most for. Of course a black bear makes noise. They are not quiet animals. The one caveat is that this black bear makes noise in an unconventional way.

"Well, it does sing. But only on rare occasion."

"It sings?"

"Yes."

"I've never heard a bear sing. What does it sound like?"

Lying Simon.

This is the moment he rehearsed with obsession. He tells himself he is being no different from his client. She is a commercial actress, and that profession requires being the spokesperson for products while not being entirely honest about their quality and convenience.

"It has a beautiful voice," he tells her. He compares the voice to Sting. This fib determines the moment he has convinced himself will restore his marriage, because what else can he do?

Ecstatic Simon.

His client says yes. She requests he submit an offer to the seller at the asking price. Simon does all he can to not leap in glee right there.

He quickly escorts Ms. Desmond to her car before the off chance the black bear decides to start singing. Nothing is in ink yet. Until agreements are signed, his marriage will not recover, so he must keep up the facade until all contracts are finalized and notarized.

Relieved Simon.

The papers are signed and his client now has the keys and deed. He deposits his commission check and runs home to the bedroom. His wife is on the bed, flipping through a family recipe book passed down to her from the time her family lived under the Tzars.

He tells her about his accomplishment. He explains to her that this means they will be able to go out and shop more. His wife gives him a sad sentiment and says, "I still feel dead inside."

Irate Simon.

He begins to berate her with a boiling face and veins pulsing in his clenched fist.

"What do you have to feel so miserable about?" he screams. "Why do you cling to a fantasy of that piss-poor country of yours? What did I pay for?"

She turns her back towards him and sinks into herself, clinging to her knees. Simon's pity is gone and an authoritarian rage consumes him.

"False advertising! That is what you are! An ungrateful whore from a sleazy catalog. Where would you be without me? I know. You'd be in some breadline or sucking some grocer off!"

She begins to respond but not in English. Her words are slow and simple, deliberately for him. Yet, despite her time in America, her husband has rejected, unconsciously or otherwise, any knowledge of her language.

"I'm doing my best to give you a better life," he says, lowering his voice.

She responds again, still mastering her own language. He prays for her to stop and to submit to his explanation. "Why do you still barely know English?" he asks her, infuriated again. "Then you would understand everything I just achieved to save our love."

She responds again on her own terms in her own tongue. She gets up and walks towards the bathroom. Simon notices she is walking taller, as if she just recovered from whatever sorrow she experienced just a few moments ago.

The bathroom door slams. The shower runs and he hears her sing a hymn from her motherland. All he can do is listen. Not only is he unable to comprehend the lyrics, but he is unable to absorb the culture.

Resentful Simon.

A cheap motel is not much of a home. Still, a hiding place is better than no home. His employer can't find him here, so he lives off the side of the highway knowing they are likely calling his house to get him back to work.

Unbeknownst to Simon, he is missing critical calls. But he needs to sulk in pity. Too bad this civilization rotates with no regard to his hopes and intentions.

Shit-Out-Of-Luck Simon.

Ms. Desmond is bringing a lawsuit against the Realtor company. She claims damages from what Simon intentionally did not disclose to her. Mainly, the black bear has caused mental distress and is affecting her ability to put the home back on the market.

The black bear sings every night. It has the voice of a screeching baboon doused in gasoline and lit on fire while mid-orgasm. The sound leaves all of Ms. Desmond's suitors running from her home with flaccid cocks and deters any developer from constructing real estate nearby to raise the property value.

Hopeless Simon.

This is unfair, he tells himself. He is an honest man with honest intentions. "Even honest men lie and I have nothing to be ashamed of" he says in a smudged mirror under a flickering light.

His job terminates him and his real estate license is suspended. He figures this is for the best. For all he knows, the next property in his portfolio could have a mango tree that shouts bigoted words every time a fruit is plucked from its branches.

Last Stand Simon.

The severity of the situation does not hit him until he sees the dollar figure Ms. Desmond is suing for, including his personal liability. Even without the lawsuit, he is out of work and near financial ruin. Life is a lie, this is what he tells himself as he sips his coffee in a McDonald's parking lot.

"It's that fucking bear," he mutters into his roasted coffee. "Or that little 19th century twat who gave a fucking bear honey."

His job won't save him, the way it didn't save his marriage.

The court of law won't save him, the way it didn't save his job.

And his civilization, or its laws, won't save him.

He drives through the valley of empty green lots where developers once envisioned constructing lucrative estates and complexes. As he drives, he can hear the black bear and its deafening songs. He thinks of his wife and her hymn in the shower. He presses more weight onto the accelerator.

The tires scratch against the curb as he pulls over to park. He sees the black bear laid on its back and howling as if he's giving an encore at Madison Square Garden. In the trunk, Simon pulls out two pans that he had previously used to furnish a kitchen in one of his properties.

A ladder is beside the house on top of the grass. He balances it against the gutter and begins to climb, using his armpits to keep possession of the two pans. With astonishing balance, he steps onto the wooden, unscratched shingles and grabs the two pots and begins banging.

"Get the fuck off the roof!" he yells. "You ruined my life you miserable fucker!"

He steps closer, banging the metal louder, creating an agitating noise. Simon escalates the noise and the black bear rises to his hind legs. He stops singing and roars with the fury of a beast in the wild. The black bear does not budge or cede ground.

Poor, Miserable Simon.

Inspiration strikes Simon in that moment. "Stay here!" he directs the black bear. "I'll be right back." He figures he can jerry-rig a flamethrower from a blowtorch and leaf-blower in his garage.

The alchemy of emotions can make any man deranged. There is no way he has the capability to create any such contraption and there is no possibility the black bear will heed Simon's demand. Before Simon can head back to the ladder, the black bear mauls him and throws the corpse down into the bed of gladiolus flowers.

I Stumble into a Home

Arabian mares.
Contained within the borders
of a picture frame.

Fluttering around.
No way out for the raven.
Inescapable.

Lacking momentum.
A slew of slugs stay dormant.
Puddles of mucus.

Determined spiders.
Patiently weaving cobwebs.
Waiting for their prey.

Floorboards creak and moan.
Should I investigate mice?
Or apparitions?

My isolation
at this home in the deep woods.
I feel a terror.

A grandfather clock.
Each swing mimics cruel laughter.
Counting to my death.

Sterling crucifix
reigning above the foyer.
I see damnation.

Eyes in the window.
Trapped inside the dusty glass.
Not my irises.

The wallpaper rips.
Leaking pipes make the walls wail.
Water stains form smiles.

A stiff wedding gown.
Draped over an ottoman.
Grass stains on the seams.

Inside the fireplace . . .
I see two figures swaying
coated in black ash.

Pair of dangling feet
Burnt from now extinguished flames.
The stench strangles me.

My breath is stolen!
Pouring mold engulfs my lungs.
Someone please help me.

The Demon from Helsinki

Like most children from Helsinki, the boy's literacy exceeded simply comprehending written words. He knew how to look for artistry woven into the collection of letters. Particularly, he had a fascination with poets and the way they constructed their messages.

He took a liking to poems about winter and the cold. "Stopping by Woods on a Snowy Evening" by Robert Frost sparked a nagging interest in him. He obsessed over the redundancy of the last two lines, "And miles to go before I sleep." None of the answers his teachers provided him as to why the line repeated could satisfy his curiosity.

"You need to give it a break for awhile," his mother told him as they walked out of the market.

"What do you think it means, mom?" the boy asked.

"This is the hundredth time you've asked me. I am not answering anymore because you insult me every time I tell you what I think."

While she had frustration with her son's persistence, she never took for granted that this was an insignificant trouble. She was frustrated at Finnish men and women who trivialized the value of literacy by forgetting that most people in the world, including the developed world, were illiterate.

The boy held onto his mother's hand as she cradled the brown paper bag that held fresh bread, lettuce, and other essentials in her other arm. The scarf wrapped around her hair kept the crisp falling flutter of snow from wetting her, the same way the boy's newsboy hat kept him dry.

"Do you know of any poems about men turning into robots?" the boy asked. "Like Kafka's Metamorphosis, but instead of a cockroach a man transforms into a machine."

"That is a very specific question. I do not. But I suppose you could write a collection."

"I could. It would probably sell millions of copies around the world. But I don't want my poems to rhyme. Some people think all poems have to rhyme, but that is not true."

"Your poems do not have to rhyme if you do not want them to rhyme."

They turned down the crowded street and continued to walk. His mother exchanged smiles with familiar faces. As they made it further down the street, she started to notice that people were looking up towards the sky. At first she did not look up with them.

"There is a new American film called '*The Phantom Creeps*.' I would like to see it. It is about a mad scientist with a giant robot and he . . ."

The boy trailed off. He felt something hit his cheeks that reminded him of kicked-up dirt on a football field; it was debris. He saw people scatter and fall over each other and at first it seemed like a silly scene in a Buster Keaton film; but they were fleeing. His ears were deafened and it was a sensation he had never experienced before. Bombs began to explode and buildings began to collapse.

Balls of fire were unleashed upon the street. The destroyed bricks resembled splashes in the ocean. Both the mother and son heard everyone screaming as they ran. The mother had a vice grip on her son's hand (it did not hurt the boy only because he was so frightened) and she dragged her son through the alleyways.

Never before had he heard his mother shriek. Never before had he heard anyone shriek the way he was hearing at this moment. It was an ugly sound, one that made his heart feel as if it would implode. The boy was not aware that he had been shrieking the whole time as well.

In the panic of it all, the boy did not recognize where they were running towards. His mother had already abandoned her grocery bag, because at that moment there was nothing more important than their survival.

They passed a man standing at a corner attempting to direct people. He was an authority figure in a tight coat and a gas mask. The eyes of the mask were large and white and his mouth was hidden. The boy had seen these types of masks before and they used to make him think of insects, but right then they made him think of demons.

With his short legs, the boy had difficulty keeping up with his mother. Even in her elevated shoes, she ran with ferocity. He tried to match the sounds he heard to the explosions he saw, but the bombs were falling too frequently now. His vision was no longer reliable due to the dust and tears caught in his eyes.

They passed a bloodied man stammering around as if he was going to fall over at any moment. As they ran by him, the boy looked up and saw that under the layers of black and gray over his face was a broken skull and ravaged flesh.

The boy continued to run and his arm felt as if it was going to rip from his shoulder. His mother picked up the speed and nothing would make her loosen her grip. They continued to run and the boy felt a quick pain in his head, like a flick of a strong finger, but he heard nothing and suddenly all was quiet and calm.

He opened his eyes with a shiver. There were no streets or roads in sight. Not a single sound pierced his ears. He stood in a foot of snow with white-capped mountains in the skyline. He looked around and there were no footprints or trails nearby. The boy had no idea of where he was or how he got there, but suddenly he no longer felt like a boy.

Wind hit his face, but the gusts were not cold. The boy felt nothing, he was only able to see and hear. He tried to take a step but he was unable to move. Like a standing statue in winter weather, he was stuck and only able to see what was in front of him.

Off in the distance, he saw vague movements as if shadows had become embodied with consciousness. His curiosity peeked and he desired to explore. He tried to move his legs again but still couldn't. Instead his body began to dematerialize. Part by part, chunk by chunk, bit by bit . . . pieces of him turned into cubes that radiated vibrant colors of rainbows before they dissolved. He witnessed himself vanish only to materialize at his intended destination.

The boy had an epiphany. There was only one way he was able to escape the bombings and take refuge in the mountains.

"I teleported myself to safety!" the boy cried out. "But how did I get this miraculous power?"

To experiment, the boy attempted to teleport again. In the same manner as before, his body transformed into a thousand tiny colorful cubes before appearing in a new location. He performed this feat dozens of times. He marveled at his own power.

"This is unbelievable," he shouted into the white void of the empty mountains.

For a moment, he stopped experimenting with his ability to look around. The scene reminded him of a poem his mother had told him about but he had never read himself. Poems that were hundreds of pages never interested him. He could not remember the poet, only that it was an Italian man that had long passed away. He did not remember what the poem was about either. All he could remember was the title and that the poem took place on a mountain that he imagined to be white.

"This is my little Purgatorio," he said, smiling to himself as the mountain made him recall the little he knew of the work. While he remembered his mother explaining that the mountain in the story was not supposed to be a pleasant place, compared to the alternative of where the boy just escaped from, his current situation was preferred.

As he continued teleporting closer to the towering mountain, he saw three figures walking towards him. They slushed through the snow and the boy stopped using his powers so he could observe them. Only when they approached closer did he recognize that they were two men and a woman. They wore white coats and masks that concealed their faces. None of them spoke and the silence frightened him.

Only the three pairs of eyes were visible, and each one displayed concern and at moments the boy thought he saw fear. He tried to ask them why they were looking at him in that manner, but he was unable to speak. The figure in the middle reached into his coat and pulled out what looked like a pen, but the object illuminated light and he pointed it directly at the boy.

In the distance, through the echoes of the mountains, he heard sobbing. The sound was too far to analyze, but he could tell it was a crying woman and it faintly resembled his mother. The boy remembered her crying like that when news of his father reached home the year prior.

The boy started to squint because the light the man shined began to hurt his eyes. The wind picked up and even though he still could not feel the cold, the weather bothered him. So he concentrated and began to break down his body again, with the attempt to transport himself as far away from these three people.

None of the three seemed to be bothered by the boy disappearing with such a colorful spectacle right in front them. This forced the boy to wonder if he was in a bizarre place or if his new powers made him evolve into something strange. He watched the figures until his eyes dissolved as part of the teleportation technique.

He reconfigured himself someplace new, far from the wintry wilderness. White walls surrounded him and the paint was so perfect and clean that it strained his sight.

Bringing himself to this new setting unsettled him. He felt as if he did not put his body back together properly. Now his figure seemed alien to him. At this point he panicked because the thought of himself no longer being human was at the forefront of his mind. He asked himself if he lost a bit of humanity each time he used his power.

Everything around him looked more indistinct and he assumed this was due to the slipping of his sanity. He asked himself, "what if this power turns me from a sentient being into some kind of animal or monster?"

He slowed his breathing to try and compose himself. With each breath, his sight was now more clear. The room became more distinct and he could see everything and everyone in front of him.

There were rows of desks and he recognized that he was standing in his classroom. Children his age occupied some of the desks but none of the students sat properly. They were all slouching with their heads hung backwards. The boy knew that if their teacher was at the head of the class, none of the students would dare sit in a disrespectful manner.

The chalkboard behind him was riddled with math problems written all across. Math was never his strongest subject, but even from first glance he knew the solution written for each problem was incorrect. Some of the formulas were incoherent to start.

Upon further examination, the boy noticed that the other children were missing some of their limbs. He had seen children with missing limbs before. One of his classmates at school was disabled. The other children nicknamed him "One-Armed Johan." Ironically, the classmate they nicknamed had both of his arms. It was the leg he was missing.

While the boy could not remember who originated the sarcastic and facetious nickname, it made him reminisce on a conversation he had with his mother one evening at the supper table.

"I want to know how he got the one leg," the boy said, sipping his evening soup.

"You already know how he got the one leg," the mother said. "He was born with it. You want to know how he lost the other leg."

At first, the boy was going to protest and complain that his mother was misunderstanding. Then he realized she was using proper grammar to instigate.

"Ha . . . Ha. Very funny," the boy said.

The mother smiled and she waited in silence for a few seconds as her smile faded. "You should not tease your friend," she said. "It is not compassionate to do so."

Back in the glaring white classroom, the boy saw a woman walking down the aisle between the desks. Despite being inside, she wore the same mask as the people along the snowy mountain side. Over each child, she leaned down and studied them before moving to the next, like a guard dog investigating on patrol.

The masked woman then turned her sights to the boy, and at first she was calm. Suddenly, her eyes turned to panic and the boy heard screaming and crying. But it was not the masked woman who was hysterical, it was a sound from afar. A great sense of shame draped the boy.

"I must have descended and become a demon," he said to himself. "That is the only explanation for these satanic powers I now have."

With the same colorful flare, the boy transported his body far away. The children and the woman began to leave his view until he was completely gone.

He did not recognize the next location. There was too much brightness for him to see. He noticed that his ability to form coherent thoughts digressed and that petrified him.

The screaming was louder than before and the voice straining itself was identical to his mother's. The boy diagnosed himself as insane and compared the situation to witnessing one's own botched surgery.

Frantically, the boy continued to break down his body and reform it in an attempt to escape the screams. He abused his ability with such rapidity, yet there was no refuge. Every time he rebuilt himself, he could see the radiant, rainbow cubes scattered all around him that displayed the remnants of his body and the trail he traveled.

His abundant use of the power became too overwhelming. He was no longer a physical being and he held on to his fading vision with such a weak grasp. All around him were the scattered pieces of himself. As the colors dissolved and the cubes disappeared, the boy realized they were not conjuring somewhere new. He became a witness to his own erasure as the blinding light took over from the spots where he faded away.

The familiar screeches continued. It was just as loud as ever. He knew it would only stop when the last of his construct was gone forever.

Notes on Previous Publication

WTMMG
originally published in *On the Run* and inspired by Nick Hakim's album "Will This Make Me Good"

A Peculiar Day in the Douro Valley
originally published in the *New Plains Review*

3 Ailments
originally published in *Querencia Press*

The high E
originally published in the *Rabble Review*

Changes or (Antonio Sánchez Saves the Day)
originally published in *Prometheus Dreaming*

_____ Simon
originally published in *Suburban Witchcraft*

The Demon from Helsinki
originally published in *East by Northeast Magazine*

Thank Yous

I want to thank all my friends and family, obviously. But I want to extend further gratitude to the following people.

Fred Wilcox and Mary Beth O'Connor, my teachers and mentors – thank you for telling a dyslexic and insecure young man that he was writer. And for all of my drafts you read, especially the terrible ones.

To my lifelong friend, Nick Hakim, whose album "Will This Make Me Good" inspired the piece "WTMMG." Thank you for letting me share this story.

My older brother Alex – as most siblings, we've had highs and lows. But you've always shown up when I've needed you.